BIG
Sticker Activity
Christmas Santa

Use the stickers at the back of this book for the activity pages. When you see a dotted shape on the page find the right sticker and put it in position. All other stickers can be used where you wish!

There are also four press-out pages and a cute fold-out scene to colour and stick lots of brilliant festive stickers on.

Skating Party

Can you match up the dancing penguins?

All Wrapped Up

Can you match up the three presents before and after they were wrapped?

One, Two, Three

Count these Christmas objects.

Write the answers in the shapes

Sleigh

Baubles

Stars

Santa's Grotto

Can you spot five differences between the two pictures of Santa in front of his workshop?

In the Snowy Forest

How many reindeers can you find?

Write the answer in the star

Decorating the Tree

Count how many bows, baubles and gingerbread men are on the tree.

Write the answers in the white ovals

Christmas Counting

Can you work out these sums?

1 + 1 =

2 + 1 =

2 + 2 =

Tree Decorating

Add some festive patterns to these baubles and colour them in.

Load It Up

Draw lines to match up the shoes to their owners.

Snap, Crack, Bang

Can you count how many red, blue and gold crackers? Write the answers in the coloured flashes.

Elf Trails

How many gifts does each elf collect on each path? Write the answer in the circles.

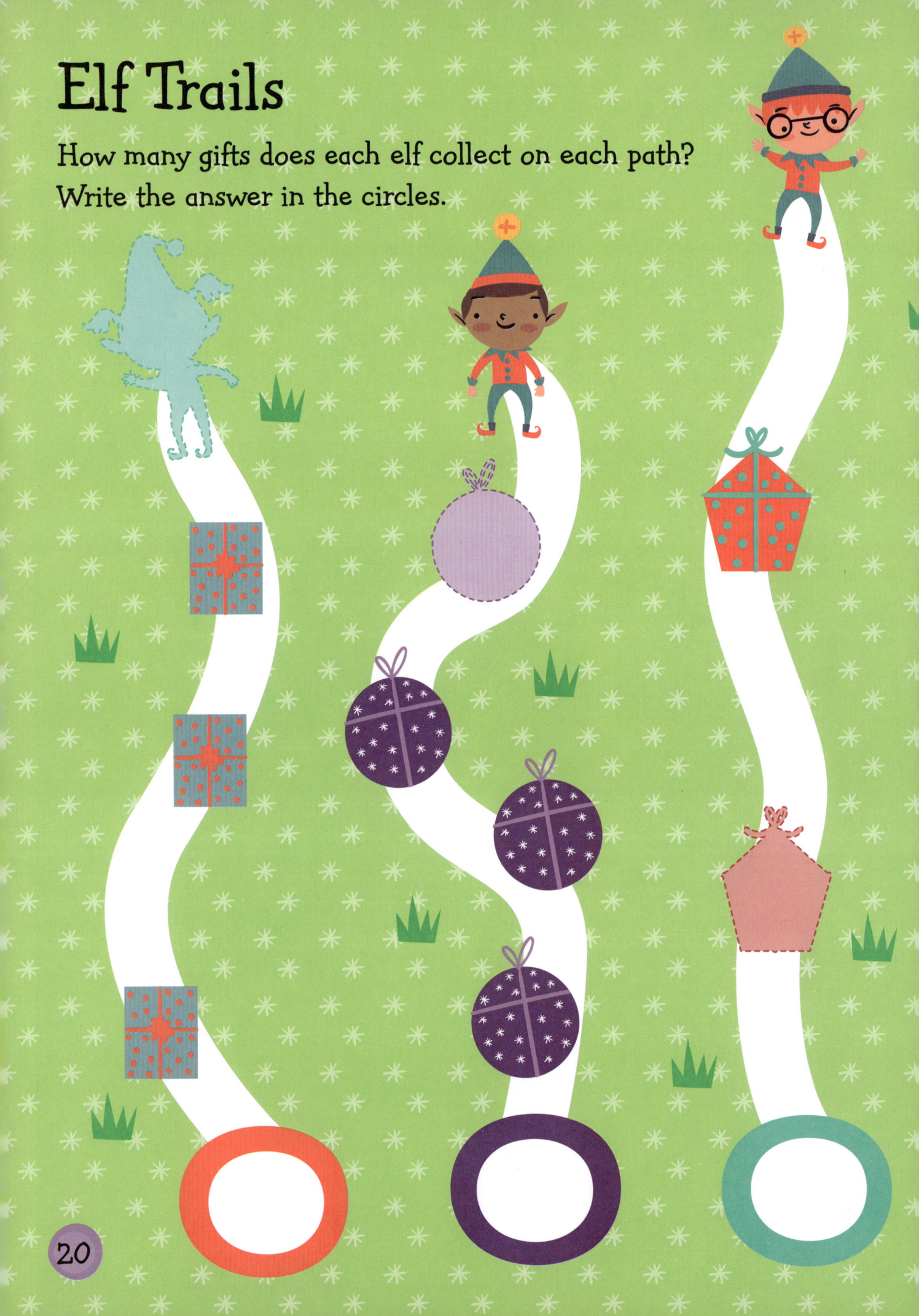

Festive Star Chain

Draw some stars, trace over and colour in to finish these Christmas chains.

Yum, Yum

Decorate these tasty biscuits with stars and swirls.

Present Mix Up

The words for these three gifts have been muddled up. Can you put the correct word on each tag?

| RAC | OOBK | RAEB |

Light Up the Room

Find the next colour light in the sequence.

Christmas Visit

Circle these objects in the scene.

Odd One Out

Can you spot the item that's slightly different in each row?

Santa's House
Finish drawing Santa's home by tracing over the lines, add stickers and colour in.

Flying Above

Can you match the coloured wings to their angel owners?

Starts with 'S'

All these items begin with the same letter - except one. Can you circle it?

Festive Wordsearch

Can you spot all the words in the grid?

TREE   HOLLY
BOW   TOY
SANTA

S	A	N	T	A
B	K	S	R	E
O	X	R	E	T
W	K	W	E	O
H	O	L	L	Y

Santa Place Cards

Push these cards out and fold on the dotted line. Fill each one in with the name of each dinner guest and place on the table.